The Wind in the Willows

BONNEY PRESS

Published by Bonney Press,
an imprint of Hinkler Books Pty Ltd
45–55 Fairchild Street
Heatherton Victoria 3202 Australia
www.hinkler.com

BONNEY
PRESS

Cover design: Jess Matthews
Illustrator: Lee Holland
Text adapted by: Katie Hewat
Design: Paul Scott and Patricia Hodges
Editorial: Emily Murray
Prepress: Splitting Image

ISBN: 978 1 4889 1295 5

Printed and bound in China

The Wind in the Willows

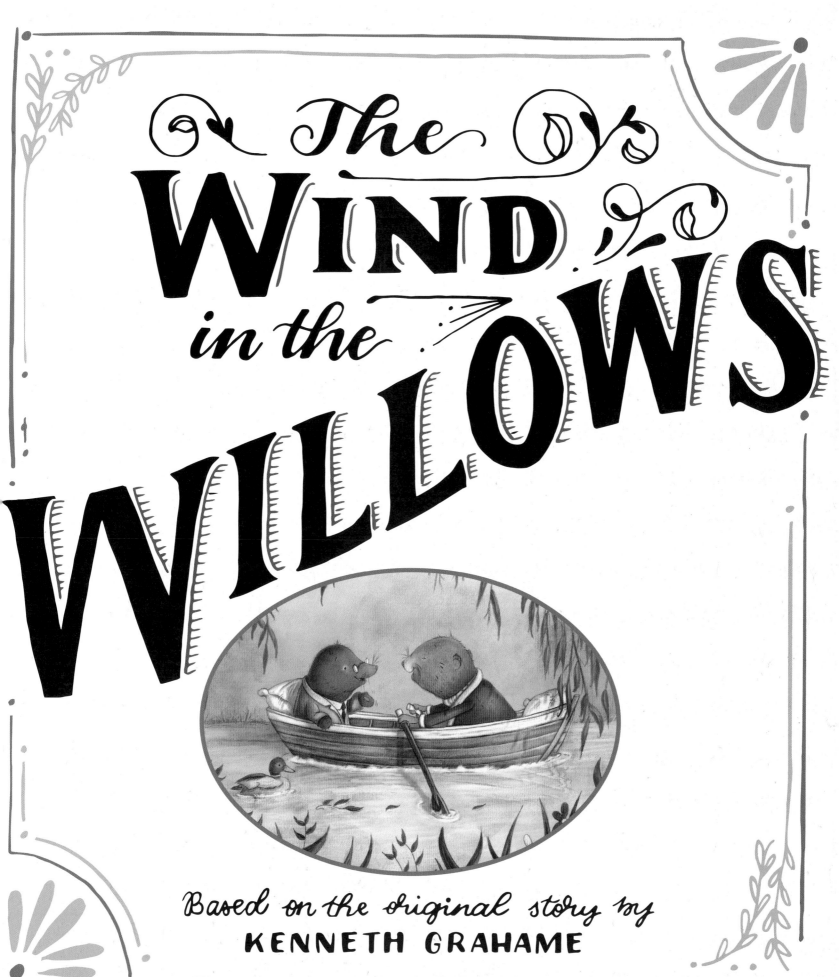

Based on the original story by
KENNETH GRAHAME

Mole had spent all morning spring-cleaning his little home. He had dust in his throat and eyes, splashes of paint over his black fur, an aching back and tired arms. Mole flung his brush on the floor. 'Hang spring-cleaning!' he said, and he marched out the front door, up the tunnel and into the sunshine.

Mole ran and tumbled through the warm grass. He ran and ran, through meadows and small woods, until he came to a wide river that was all a-shake and a-shiver, glinting in the sun. He sat down by the bank, fascinated. Mole had never travelled this far from home, and he'd never seen a river. He didn't feel at all guilty about leaving his spring-cleaning behind.

Just then, Mole saw a dark hole in the opposite bank. In that hole, looking back at him, were two bright eyes! Mole waved and soon a little brown creature with a friendly face and long whiskers emerged. It was a water rat!

'Hello, Mole,' said the water rat.

'Hello, Rat,' replied Mole.

'Would you like to come over?' asked Rat.

'I sure would!' said Mole.

Rat got into a little green boat and rowed across the river. Mole climbed in – a rather tricky business as Mole's short arms and legs made this quite difficult. Rat pulled and heaved until eventually Mole tumbled over the side and they both fell in a heap at the bottom of the boat, giggling.

Rat began to row and Mole felt he'd never been so happy in his life. 'What a wonderful day this is!' he said.

Rat agreed. 'Believe me,' he said, 'there is nothing better than simply messing about in boats. Shall we make a day of it?'

'Oh, yes please!' replied Mole.

Before they set off, Rat stopped at his house and climbed back on board with a large basket. 'What's inside?' asked Mole.

'Oh, just cold chicken,' replied Rat, rowing away from the bank, 'and a leg of ham, cold beef, fruit salad, bread rolls, sandwiches, ginger beer, lemonade, chocolate cake …'

Mole couldn't believe his ears. What a feast! He trailed a paw in the water and daydreamed until they bumped gently against the riverbank.

They had a delightful lunch, watching the activity on the busy river. At one point, Rat waved as his good friend Toad passed by in a brand-new rowboat.

Mole thought it was a wonderful boat. 'Oh, it won't last long,' replied Rat. 'Toad will crash it or break it, and by this time next week he'll have a new toy or hobby. Toad is a very fine fellow but he's quite irresponsible, and a terrible braggart.'

Rat regaled Mole with Toad's adventures for the rest of the afternoon. When it was time to leave, Rat invited Mole to stay at his house for a while. Mole was delighted – Rat had even promised to teach him to row and to swim. What grand adventures the fast friends would have!

One bright summer morning, Mole said, 'Ratty, can I ask you a favour?'

'Of course my dear fellow,' replied Rat, who was splashing in the river.

'Would you take me to see Toad? I would so like to meet him.'

'Certainly!' said Rat. 'Let's get the boat and set out at once. Toad's always happy to have visitors.'

And indeed, Toad was. He rushed out to meet them on the rolling green lawn. 'Welcome to Toad Hall!' he called, waving his arm towards the sprawling brick mansion.

Mole told Toad how much he admired Toad Hall. 'It's the finest house on the river, isn't it?' boasted Toad. 'In fact, it's the finest house anywhere!'

Mole asked Toad how he was enjoying his new boat. 'Oh, boats-shmoats!' replied Toad. 'I'm over boats. I have a new passion – caravanning!'

Toad excitedly dragged them to show off his very fancy new caravan. 'Tomorrow I am taking off on a long journey. I might be gone weeks, or even years! You should join me,' he suggested.

Rat quickly thanked Toad but declined his invitation. He had been on adventures with Toad before, and they never turned out well.

After a lovely day, Mole and Rat headed home, wishing Toad happy travels.

One day, Rat was teaching Mole to swim when there was a rustle in the bushes and a striped head appeared.

'Oh, hello Badger!' called Rat. 'Won't you come and join us?' But the creature quickly disappeared without saying a word.

Mole was puzzled until Rat explained that Badger was very shy. This made Mole very curious to meet Badger, so he asked Rat if they could visit him. 'We simply can't. Badger lives in the Wild Wood, which is a dark and unfriendly place,' warned Rat.

At first Mole accepted this but, as the days wore on and winter arrived, he felt he absolutely had to meet Badger. One afternoon while Rat was resting, Mole slipped out and headed for the Wild Wood. The wind was blowing, and the Wood was very dark and gloomy, especially as night began to set in.

Mole began to feel quite scared. There were glowing eyes staring at him from trees and bushes, and suddenly a rabbit rushed past him. 'Get out of here!' the rabbit cried. 'The Wild Wood is full of dangerous stoats and weasels!'

Mole began to panic. He ran about blindly, tripping over tree roots and crashing into other creatures until he found a hollow in an old tree. He crept inside, shivering and shaking and wishing he'd listened to Rat.

Back home, Rat had awoken from his nap to find Mole missing. He looked outside and saw footprints in the snow leading to the Wild Wood. Rat knew exactly where Mole had gone. He pulled on a warm coat, lit a lantern and headed out to find his friend.

Rat followed the footprints all through the Wood until he reached the tree hollow. He held the lantern up and found Mole inside, terrified but safe.

'Oh, Moly!' said Rat. 'I was terribly worried. Let's get you home.' But it had started snowing, so when they tried to retrace their footsteps, they found the snow had covered them over. Mole and Rat were helplessly lost.

They blundered through the cold, wet snow for hours. 'Oh, we're going to freeze out here if starvation doesn't get us first!' cried Mole. 'And only if we don't get carried off by wild creatures!'

Mole grew so tired that his little legs could scarcely carry him and he tripped over a stone. As he sat in the cold snow rubbing his shin, Rat suddenly let out a whoop of delight.

'Well done Moly!' Rat cried. 'You've stumbled onto Badger's doorstep!' They cleared the snow from around the doorstep and soon came to a small green door and a bell, which Rat happily rang. They heard slow footsteps approaching the door and it eventually opened just wide enough to a reveal a long snout and a pair of sleepy eyes.

'Badger! Please let us in! It's me, Water Rat, and my new friend Mole. We're lost in the snow.'

'Ratty, my dear little man!' exclaimed Badger. 'Come in at once. You must be freezing.'

Inside, Badger sat Rat and Mole in front of the fire and gave them warm dressing gowns, slippers and cups of hot chocolate. As they warmed through, Badger asked them what was new on the riverbank.

'Oh, it's much the same,' replied Rat. 'Toad has given up caravanning and taken up driving motor cars. He really is the worst driver – he's crashed seven cars already! It won't be long before someone gets hurt.'

'Well, we can't be expected to do anything strenuous, or heroic or even moderately active during winter,' said Badger, yawning. 'But I tell you what, Ratty. When the weather is warmer, we'll go to Toad and make him see sense. But now it's bedtime.'

Soon the snow cleared and the sun peeked out from behind the clouds. It was spring once more.

One morning, Badger arrived at Rat's house. 'It's time to pay Toad a visit,' he announced. 'He has just bought himself a new, very powerful motor car. We must convince him to give up his dangerous ways.'

The three friends set off to Toad Hall and spotted the shiny new car parked outside. Toad flung open the front door cheerfully.

'Hello, hello!' he shouted. 'Have you come to see my new motor car? I do believe it is the most splendid car in the whole world. You're just in time for a drive!'

'It seems we are just in time, but not for a drive,' said Badger. He dragged Toad inside to the study. After a while, they came back out and Badger announced that Toad had agreed to change his irresponsible ways and give up motor cars forever.

Toad wriggled and writhed for a moment, then cried, 'I won't! I love driving! It's so much fun and I'll drive as fast as I like!'

Badger angrily told Toad he would have to stay in his room until he saw reason, and confiscated Toad's car keys. Later that day, when the house had gone quiet, Toad climbed out the window and down the drainpipe. He ran until he came to a small town where he saw a shiny motor car parked by the road. The keys were inside! Toad couldn't help himself – he climbed in, started the engine, and took off with a screech. He was soon out in the countryside with the engine roaring and the wind whipping past. He was so happy! At least, that is, until disaster struck.

A few days later, Toad found himself in court in handcuffs, charged with stealing a motor car, driving dangerously and crashing into a ditch. Toad was convinced he would simply be given a fine, but the stern judge had something else in mind.

'I sentence you to twenty years in jail!' he boomed.

Toad was shocked and, all of a sudden, very sorry for his bad behaviour.

'I'm sorry!' he wailed. 'Take pity on a poor Toad who didn't know any better!' But it was too late. The guards dragged him away and locked him in a cold, grey cell.

Days passed and Toad felt very sorry for himself indeed. How he wished he had listened to his friends! 'Wise Badger, clever Rat, sensible Mole,' he said to himself. 'You tried to save me from myself but I wouldn't listen. I swear, if I ever get out of here, I will be a much better Toad!'

Toad sounded so sad and sorry that the jailor's daughter, who often brought food to the prisoners, felt terribly bad for him and offered to help him escape. Toad was overjoyed, and ever so thankful.

The girl brought Toad some clothes to disguise himself so that he could sneak out. Toad thought he might dress as a great lord, but was very disappointed when he found he was to dress as a washerwoman. The girl helped him pull on a long dress, an apron and a bonnet that covered most of his face, and when all was in place, Toad slipped out to make his escape.

The runaway washerwoman headed for the station and boarded the next train. Toad sat down and chuckled to himself. 'What an extraordinary Toad I am!' he thought to himself. 'Who else but me could escape from such a place!'

But soon enough, Toad was in hot water again: he could hear sirens following the train and he knew that the police would catch up to him. 'What a silly Toad I am,' he wailed, panicking. 'Of course the police would find me here! What am I to do?'

Toad needed to get off without being seen, so he waited until the train went through a tunnel, and jumped out on the other side. He landed with a crash and tumbled down the hill into a bush. The sirens passed without slowing, and Toad realised he wasn't going to get caught. He brushed himself off, then skipped along, singing a song he'd just made up called 'What a Clever Toad Am I'.

After a while, Toad came to a river. He followed it, still dressed as a washerwoman and singing away. Soon he heard the clip-clopping of a horse walking along the riverbank behind him. It was pulling a barge along the river. Toad felt quite tired, and fancied a comfortable ride on the barge. He asked the woman steering it if he could come aboard.

'Do you have money to pay for your passage?' she asked.

'Alas, I do not!' he cried in a high-pitched voice. 'I am just a poor washerwoman. Do take pity on me!'

The woman guided the barge to the bank and Toad hopped on.

Toad was quite pleased with himself until he realised that the woman had absolutely no intention of giving him a free ride.

'Lucky for you,' the woman said to Toad, 'I have a gigantic, enormous, stupendous pile of laundry below deck that needs washing. Hop to it!' And she gave him a little shove down a short staircase.

Toad would never dream of doing such hard work, so he decided to take a nap on the washing pile. Soon enough, the woman found him fast asleep.

She flew into a rage. 'Lazy cheat!' the woman cried. She pushed Toad up the stairs, picked him up and threw him straight over the side! He landed in the river with a huge splash.

Toad coughed and spluttered and kicked and paddled until he reached the bank. He was a soggy mess, and now he was really quite furious. He hopped up and down and shook his fist in the air. 'I'll teach you to mess with the famous Mr. Toad!' he shouted.

He ran along the riverbank until he caught up with the barge horse. Ignoring the woman's angry cries, he untied the horse, mounted it, and galloped away, laughing like a madman as he sang his latest ditty, 'Ain't No Better Toad than Toad'.

But Toad soon found that a horse without a saddle makes for quite a tender backside, so he decided to set the horse free. He climbed down, rubbing his sore bottom and continued along the river on foot.

By now, the light was beginning to fade and Toad was tired and hungry. He didn't want to spend the night out in the open and began to worry. 'Why, oh why do dreadful things always happen to poor Toad?' he asked himself, plopping down on a rock beside the river.

Just then a motor car came along the road beside the river. Two men in the car saw someone who they took to be a poor washerwoman beside the road and pulled over to see if they could help.

'Oh, thank you, kind gentlemen,' said Toad in his high-pitched washerwoman's voice, and they were soon travelling down the road. But the driver wasn't going fast enough for Toad's liking, so he asked, 'Would you be so kind as to allow me to drive? I have always dreamed of driving a motor car.' The men thought this an odd request, but they were polite fellows, so they agreed.

But once Toad was behind the wheel, he was a menace! He took off, speeding around corners so fast that two wheels lifted off the ground. The men were terrified, holding on for dear life and yelling for Toad to slow down. Eventually, Toad's bonnet blew off his head.

'You!' cried one of the shocked men. 'You're that escaped prisoner!'

'Yes, it is I, Toad!' said Toad, 'The motor-car snatcher, the prison breaker, the Toad who always escapes!' The men tried to grab Toad, but he suddenly pulled hard on the steering wheel, sending the car right over the edge of the riverbank. Toad was flung high and far, landing on the other side of the river.

He stood on the far bank watching the men struggling out of the river and began to giggle – as much as they might try, no one got the better of Toad! Toad realised he had almost made it to Ratty's house, so he tramped along merrily, composing a new song called 'Ode to Toad'.

Toad was overjoyed when he found his good friends Mole and Ratty at home, and they were most relieved to see their friend safe and well. Toad told them how he'd outsmarted everyone who was after him and he'd even begun to sing one of his new songs when Ratty cut him short.

'Enough!' said Rat. 'Stop bragging, go upstairs and change out of those ridiculous clothes. Come back down looking like a gentleman, if you can. Then we should talk.'

Toad was very surprised at Ratty's tone, but he did what he was told, mumbling under his breath about someone being a bossy-boots.

When Toad came back downstairs, Mole gave him a plate of supper. Rat looked very serious. 'From what you've told me, you've been handcuffed, imprisoned, terrified out of your mind, starved, chased and flung into a river,' he said. 'And all because you just had to steal a motor car. What is there to be proud of?'

Toad could see Rat's point when he put it like that. He felt quite foolish and promised Rat and Mole he would not mess about with motor cars again. He felt very tired and told them he was going home to sleep in his own bed.

Mole sighed sadly, and Rat said, 'Oh dear, Toady, haven't you heard? The weasels and ferrets have taken over Toad Hall, and they refuse to leave.'

It made Toad angry to think of his beautiful house overrun by wild creatures, eating his food, touching his things and sleeping in his bed. 'I must take it back!' he said.

Just then there was a knock on the door, and Mole opened it to find Badger outside. He came in and shook Toad's hand firmly. 'My dear Toady,' he said, 'I'm so glad to see you safe and well! But what are we going to do about this Toad Hall business?' Toad was very relieved that his friends were willing to help, and the four creatures spent the evening hatching a plan.

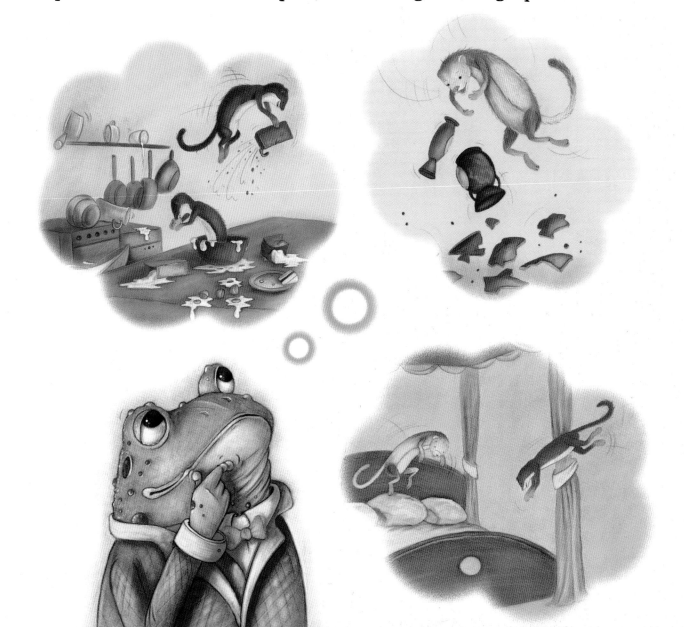

The following evening, the Chief Weasel was throwing a birthday party at Toad Hall. Badger thought this would be the perfect opportunity to sneak into Toad's house. They crept to the edge of the property and Toad guided them through a secret underground passage into the cellar, directly below the banquet hall. Each of them carried a long stick to fight off the wild creatures once they were inside.

'Right,' said Badger when they reached the cellar. 'Once we're up the stairs, we'll burst into the hall and take them by surprise.'

'Then we'll whack 'em and whack 'em and whack 'em!' cried Toad, hopping up and down. 'Let's go!'

The four friends rushed into the banquet hall, screaming and squawking and waving their sticks around. The weasels, stoats and ferrets were so surprised at the raucous display that they thought a whole army had invaded the hall. They dropped their food and dashed out of Toad Hall as fast as their legs could carry them!

Ratty, Badger, Mole and Toad all cheered, then rewarded themselves by finishing the banquet.

From that day forwards, Toad was a changed creature. He sent money and letters of thanks for their help and apologies for his poor behaviour to the jailor's daughter, the lady from the barge and the two gentlemen whose car he crashed. He even kept his promise and never drove a motor car again.

Toad always had to try very hard not to brag, but at least he did try. And he only ever sang his newest song, 'Toad the Wise and Wonderful', when he thought nobody could hear. Badger, Rat and Mole who, in fact, heard him quite often, smiled to themselves as they went about their happy, peaceful lives.